The Dark

Charlotte Jones' first play, *Airswimming*, was premiered at the Battersea Arts Centre, London and later broadcast on Radio 4. *In Flame* was premiered in January 1999 at the Bush Theatre, London, and revived at the New Ambassadors, London, in September 2000. *Martha, Josie and the Chinese Elvis* premiered at the Bolton Octagon in April 1999 and transferred to the Liverpool Everyman in May of that year. It won the *Manchester Evening News* Best Play Award of 1999. It was recently revived at the Watford Palace Theatre. Charlotte Jones won the Critics' Circle Award for Most Promising Playwright in 2000 for *In Flame* and *Martha, Josie and the Chinese Elvis*. Her most recent play, *Humble Boy*, was awarded the Susan Smith Blackburn Award 2001, the Critics' Circle Best New Play Award, 2002, and the People's Choice Best New Play Award, 2002. It opened at the Cottesloe Theatre in August 2001 before transferring to the West End, where it ran for nine months. It has since enjoyed productions all over the world.

by the same author

plays
IN FLAME
MARTHA, JOSIE AND THE CHINESE ELVIS
HUMBLE BOY

CHARLOTTE JONES
The Dark

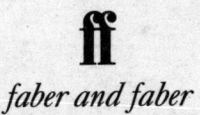

First published in 2004
by Faber and Faber Limited
3 Queen Square London WC1N 3AU

Typeset by Country Setting, Kingsdown, Kent CT14 8ES
Printed in England by Mackays of Chatham plc, Chatham, Kent

All rights reserved
© Charlotte Jones, 2004

The right of Charlotte Jones to be identified as author
of this work has been asserted in accordance with Section 77
of the Copyright, Designs and Patents Act 1988

All rights whatsoever in this work, amateur or professional,
are strictly reserved. Applications for permission for any use
whatsoever, including performance rights, must be made in advance,
prior to any such proposed use, to Peters, Fraser and Dunlop Ltd,
Drury House, 34–43 Russell Street, London WC2B 5HA.
No performance may be given unless a licence has first
been obtained.

*This book is sold subject to the condition that it shall not,
by way of trade or otherwise, be lent, resold, hired out
or otherwise circulated without the publisher's prior consent
in any form of binding or cover other than that in which
it is published and without a similar condition including
this condition being imposed on the subsequent purchaser*

A CIP record for this book
is available from the British Library

ISBN 0-571-22434-2

For Paul

The Dark was first performed at the Donmar Warehouse, London, on 18 March 2004. The cast was as follows:

Barnaby Matt Bardock
Janet Brid Brennan
Louisa Anastasia Hille
Brian Roger Lloyd Pack
John Stuart McQuarrie
Elsie Siân Phillips
Josh Andrew Turner

Director Anna Mackmin
Designer Lez Brotherston
Lighting Designer David Hersey
Sound Designer Gareth Fry

The text that follows went to press while rehearsals were still in progress, and may therefore differ in some respects from the play as performed.

Characters

John

Louisa

Barnaby

Janet

Brian

Elsie

Josh

THE DARK

SCENE ONE

Music.

The set should represent the interior of a typical terraced street of two-up, two-down houses. Six rooms, divided loosely by paper-thin walls. The six rooms represent in a highly stylised way both the rooms of one house and three houses in a row (i.e., the characters will use all the rooms as if they were their own, if necessary walking through occupied rooms without seeing the other occupants). Perhaps the 'rooms' are on different levels, accessed by a few stairs. There is a BATHROOM *– a shower fixed to a wall with a semi-perspex screen, a washbasin.* BEDROOM ONE *– a double bed, bedside table and a cot.* BEDROOM TWO *– twin beds, a TV. A* LOUNGE *– a sofa, a TV. A* KITCHEN *– a fridge, a microwave, a table, a cutlery drawer, a sink, a work surface. A* DINING ROOM-CUM-STUDY *– a computer work-station, a music system, a window. The furniture should be minimal and stylised. The rooms light up consecutively and remain lit.*

The BATHROOM *lights up. John, a man in his late thirties stands in his pyjama bottoms. His right arm is in a sling, and there are some week-old cuts and bruises on his face. He faces the audience. He is cleaning his teeth as if into the shaving mirror, with his left hand – and therefore with some difficulty. He goes on to attempt to floss one-handed.*

A moment then –

The KITCHEN *lights up. The light from an open fridge. A middle-aged (mid- to late forties) woman – Janet –*

stands at the fridge, looking in. She is brunette, not unattractive, thin but tired-looking. She looks round, as if she has forgotten what she is looking for – then looks back and takes a convenience meal on a plate and heats it in the microwave. She watches it revolve, in a daze.

A moment, then –

BEDROOM ONE *lights up. A double bed. In the corner a Moses basket. A baby monitor with a night light and a baby light revolves – images of the ocean, fishes, etc., throwing patterns on the ceiling. A woman in her midthirties – Louisa – puts a swaddled baby in its cot. A man of the same age appears behind her – her husband Barnaby. He watches her with intensity. He does not say anything. She turns round and whispers, 'Shsh.' She places the baby down with painstaking slowness. He continues to stand there.*

A moment, then –

BEDROOM TWO *lights up. Brian, Janet's husband (in his late forties/early fifties) sits in his shirt with his trousers off, socks still on, half-undressed. He has a morose quality. He is reading a tabloid paper. He stops, puts it down. He checks under the bed – takes out a hammer, then painstakingly places it back under the bed. He takes it out again as if he were going to strike someone – he is checking the speed of his reactions in an emergency situation.*

A moment, then –

The LOUNGE *lights up. An old woman – Elsie, John's seventy-year-old mother, sits with a tray on her lap, eating a boiled egg slowly. A standard lamp next to her. She pauses, looks at the contents of her spoon. She takes a magnifying glass next to her, examines the mouthful more closely. Finds nothing of note. Puts it to her mouth, eats without pleasure.*

A moment, then –

The STUDY *lights up. A teenage boy of fourteen – Josh – sits at a computer. An anglepoise lamp on the desk beside him. He is in a chat room. He types furiously at the keyboard. Then he reads the response, sniggers, types something back. He continues in this vein. There is something unnerving about him.*

All six cells are lit.

The baby starts to cry. Josh goes to his music system, turns down the music – listens to the baby. A beat. Afterwards John drops his floss. Then the microwave pings in the kitchen. An e-mail arrives on the computer. All the characters speak/type at once, and as such their words are indistinguishable:

John Bugger this buggering arm.

Louisa I told you to be quiet.

Barnaby I was only breathing!

Janet Josh! Your dinner's ready!

Brian That's it. Just in case.

Elsie This doesn't taste right.

Josh taps something out on the keyboard.

There is a sudden surge in energy – the light in each cell intensifies. Then the light flickers – a dramatic flicker . . . All the characters in each cell stop what they are doing and look around or get up, or bang the light, the computer. The lights flicker again. They are all found in varying states of bewilderment. The baby stops crying. The music stops.

The light normalises. Then it starts to fade on all the rooms except the KITCHEN, BEDROOM TWO *and the* STUDY. *Brian, who feels better now he has held his hammer, stretches and then puts on a pair of comfy trousers for the evening. Then he picks up his paper and walks into the kitchen. As he leaves the room the light fades on* BEDROOM TWO. *At the same time, Janet picks up the plate of food and walks through the other rooms to outside the* STUDY. *She does not enter. She goes as if to knock on the door, but thinks better of it. Josh continues to tap away at the computer. Janet stands with the plate.*

Janet Josh! I've got your dinner here.

Josh stops tapping but does not answer. Janet waits a moment, listens.

I hope it's all right.

Pause.

I'll just leave it here, then.

She puts it on the floor outside the room. A pause, and then Josh starts tapping away again at the computer. Janet pauses an extra moment and then goes away. Josh listens to her retreat. She goes back into the kitchen. Brian is already there. He is looking in the fridge. Josh stops tapping away and listens to make sure that his mother has retreated.

I left Josh his tea.

Brian Did he say anything?

Janet No, but I could tell he was listening. What do you want?

Brian Don't think I'll bother. I don't feel right.

Janet What's wrong with you? There's nothing wrong with you.

Brian My stomach's playing up.

Janet Oh, come on, get out of the way, I've got to make Josh's pud. Then I'll make you a sandwich.

She gets a crème brûlée out of the fridge. Then she gets a large blowtorch out of the drawer, lights it and caramelises the top of the dessert. Brian picks up his tabloid paper and starts to read it. After Janet has finished the crème brûlée she gets out a large kitchen knife and makes a cheese sandwich.

As they are thus occupied, we see Josh come out of his room and take the food. He goes back into the room and during the rest of the scene he proceeds to shovel the food down.

The lights went funny. Just now.

Brian Mmm?

Janet Flickered and then came back on.

Brian It's probably the wiring.

Janet It might be the mains.

Brian It'll be the wiring.

Janet Perhaps it's to do with voltage.

Brian You don't know what you're talking about, woman.

Janet Do you think the whole street's affected? Maybe it's not just us.

Brian I doubt it.

Janet Do you think it happened next door?

Brian How would I know? I can't see through walls.

Janet Oh, I meant to tell you. She's had the baby.

Brian What?

Janet Next door. I saw them coming home with it.

Brian Oh.

Janet I've got that old woman's number.

Brian What old woman?

Janet Other side. I could ring her.

Brian The weirdo and his mother.

Janet Yes.

Brian We're not ringing them.

Janet See if their lights went funny.

Brian I don't care if their lights went funny.

Janet No, perhaps you're right.

Brian I'm telling you. It'll just be a dodgy connection.

Janet Will you get someone in, then?

Pause.

We can't do without power.

Pause. Janet looks towards the STUDY.

The other night I heard him talking. I'm sure I did. But not to us. He wasn't talking to us.

Brian takes this in, doesn't respond. Pause.

Brian Man here slaughtered his family. Butchered them.

Janet Oh no!

Brian Execution-style killing.

Janet Oh no!

Brian Hammer to the back of their heads.

Janet No.

Brian While they were sleeping.

Janet How awful.

Brian Wife and three kids. Two boys and a girl.

Janet Oh dear.

Brian Youngest was twelve.

Janet Girl or boy?

Brian Girl. Casey.

Janet I thought Casey was a boy's name.

Brian No, girl.

Janet Ttt. I don't know.

Pause. Josh finishes eating and puts the plate back outside the door. He returns to the computer – looks at some images on his screen.

Brian Then he hanged himself.

Pause.

Took pills, covered his head with a bag and hung himself.

Pause.

Janet He wanted to die, then.

Brian He stayed twenty-four hours in the house with them all dead in their beds. Ate his breakfast, with them all dead in their beds.

Janet Why did he do that?

Brian Doesn't say.

Janet Oh dear. They were all dead and he just wandered about the house?

Brian Yes.

Janet Ate his breakfast?

Brian A bowl of porridge.

Janet Oh dear.

Brian Just shows you.

Janet (*wiping her hands*) I hope we don't need complete rewiring.

Brian I can't do anything about it tonight.

Janet Here you are. (*She passes him the sandwich.*) I'll go and see if he's finished.

She leaves. She goes to the STUDY. *She sees the plate on the floor. She sighs. She stands there.*

I've done you a pudding. Your favourite. It's still in the kitchen. Shall I get it for you?

Pause.

Have you gone to bed?

Pause.

Are you asleep?

Pause.

Have you turned into a tree?

Mother and son listen to each other. In the KITCHEN, *Brian abandons his half-eaten sandwich on the table and gets up and goes to the* BATHROOM. *As he does, he passes John, who goes into* BEDROOM TWO, *takes out the hammer that is under the bed and considers it, checks that he can use it with one arm, sighs at this state of affairs. Brian, in the* BATHROOM, *washes his face and hands, cleans his teeth during the next.*

SCENE TWO

BEDROOM ONE. *Light fades up on Barnaby and Louisa. A double bed. Louisa getting into bed.*

Barnaby Is she asleep?

Louisa Yes.

Barnaby Is she breathing?

Louisa I don't know! She was breathing a moment ago. Why don't you look this time?

Barnaby goes to the cot. He takes a mirror out, places it to the baby's mouth, looks.

Janet All right, love?

Louisa Is she?

Janet All right?

Barnaby She's all right.

Janet Sorry.

Barnaby Sorry.

Janet waits for a response, then takes the tray into the KITCHEN, *where she clears up.*

Louisa She's breathing. It is inevitable. She breathes inevitably.

Barnaby Yes . . . Sometimes I'd like someone else to breathe for me. Just for a short while.

Louisa What are you talking about?

Barnaby The effort of breathing. Once you start thinking about it.

Louisa Don't be sick. I'm going to sleep. I'm taking a pill. (*doing so*)

Barnaby Are you sure? . . . What if you don't wake up?

Louisa (*tense*) I'll wake up.

Barnaby Are we going to bed, then? (*He looks at his watch.*) It's (*the actual time*). It's only (*actual time*).

Pause.

My old one told you the date.

Louisa Sshshh.

Barnaby Have you eaten?

Louisa I had a boiled egg.

Barnaby When was that?

Louisa I don't know. Just before I fed her. I ate it quickly and without enjoyment. If you really want to know, it tasted of nothing. At least, it didn't taste of egg. Why? Are you compiling a crime report?

Barnaby I just wondered. I didn't see you eat, that's all.

Louisa You were obsessively checking on our sleeping child, that is why.

Barnaby I'm just making sure.

Louisa Goodnight.

Barnaby Louisa. We should discuss her name. She's nearly three weeks old. It just doesn't feel right. Her not having a name.

Louisa Please keep your agendas to yourself. I am trying to sleep.

Barnaby What about Rosa?

Louisa No.

Barnaby What's wrong with Rosa?

Louisa When the time comes, we'll know what her name is. Why don't you have a shower? Relax you?

Barnaby I am relaxed.

Louisa You haven't slept for two weeks! You've got to go back to work tomorrow.

Barnaby I'm not going back to work.

Louisa Don't be ridiculous.

Barnaby I'll set up on my own. I'll work from home.

Louisa I'm not talking about this now.

Barnaby But what if we don't know? I mean, what if the name doesn't present itself? We'll have to make a decision then, won't we?

Louisa Barnaby! Why can't you let me sleep? I need to sleep. I need to sleep for a hundred years! I can't decide anything until you let me sleep. (*She throws herself back down on her pillow.*)

Barnaby It's not right.

She does not answer.

SCENE THREE

Lights up on the LOUNGE. *Elsie sits before her eggshell. She has her eyes closed. John* (*who has placed the hammer back under the bed*) *leaves* BEDROOM TWO *and enters the* LOUNGE.

In BEDROOM ONE *Barnaby goes to the Moses basket. He leans over to the baby to see if she is breathing.*

Louisa Stop that.

John I've come to check on you.

Elsie makes no response.

Barnaby I'm just checking her. I have to check her.

John For all the thanks I get.

Louisa Don't wake her up, for Christ's sake.

John Mum? Are you asleep?

Barnaby She's asleep.

Louisa Turn the light off.

He does so. The baby night light remains on. He sits over the basket in a silent vigil.

Elsie The lights went off.

Barnaby You will have a name, baby. Some day soon.

John goes to take up her plate. Elsie shoos him away.

Elsie Don't crowd me!

John Had your tea?

Elsie The lights went off. Halfway through my egg.

John The bulb must be worn out.

Elsie looks at her eggshell.

Elsie They inject eggs with poison. You used to be all right with things like eggs . . . and oranges. Things with an outer skin. But not any more. They take all the goodness out. You used to be able to taste the goodness. Nothing has got any goodness in it any more.

John You could go organic.

Elsie Huh! I wasn't born yesterday . . . Look at that sling. Is that what they gave you at the hospital? That's a health hazard. You could catch something off that. The

MRI bug. Eats your flesh alive. This man. I read about it. Half his face missing.

John How inconvenient.

Elsie What?

John You're all right, then?

Elsie Of course I'm all right. Why have you got your pyjamas on already?

John I thought they'd be more comfortable.

Elsie More comfortable for what?

There is the noise of shouts outside the window. Barnaby gets up and looks out in BEDROOM ONE, *as do Janet in the* KITCHEN *and Brian in the* BATHROOM.

Here we go. I don't get a moment's peace. I didn't think I'd end my days like this.

John Just ignore it.

John looks out towards the street, troubled. Brian goes from the BATHROOM *to* BEDROOM TWO. *He lies on the bed and switches the TV on. The news plays quietly. Barnaby goes into the* BATHROOM, *crossing Brian, stares at himself in the mirror. He washes his face and hands, freshens himself up. All the actions of a very tired man. Louisa stares at her sleeping child in a detached way. Josh gets up and looks out. Possibly he joins in the shouting, or just smiles at the rumpus.*

Elsie This street never used to be like this. Everyone looked out for everyone else. You didn't need neighbourhood-watching schemes. You looked after your own, that's what you did. Now I don't know half of them. Sooner gouge their eyes out than look at you. Cut out their tongues rather than give you the time of day. There's a new lot next door – had a baby – in the old days they'd have brought it round so I could cross its palm with silver. Now they won't even take my sherbet lemons – that boy next door, just stared me in the face, wouldn't take one. There's something not right with him – he walks sideways, always has. Autistic, I wouldn't wonder. That's what they have these days, isn't it, when they're daft in the head? They can't show affection but they can see in the dark. I don't know what the world's coming to. Are you listening to me? John? John!

John What?

Elsie Go and tell them you're not a child molester. Go on.

John There's no point.

Elsie That's just like you! You won't stand up for yourself.

John I've tried it before. They don't listen.

Elsie Tell them you're not on the register. Show them the certificate from the police.

John I'd rather jump into a pit of snakes.

Elsie Tell them it was a case of mistaken identity. Tell them to mind their own business.

John What part of 'there's no point' do you not understand?

Elsie If you won't I will.

John It's just kids. Anyway, they're stopping.

Elsie What if they attack you again?

John I told you. It's just kids messing.

Elsie Kids with horns.

John They don't mean anything by it.

Elsie Look at the state of you. Have you rung the police yet?

John They can't do anything. Shall I see you into bed?

Elsie It's only (*actual time*) . . . Go on, ring them.

More shouting. He gets up, looks out of the window.

They're shouting again.

John I'm not deaf, Mother.

Elsie They're there to help you. Aren't you going to ring them then?

He picks the phone up, pretends to dial. We continue to hear the dialling tone throughout the conversation. At the same time Janet exits the kitchen, having cleaned it, and put Brian's half-eaten sandwich into the fridge. She heads for BEDROOM TWO.

John Hello. This is John Wrentmore. Yes. No, nothing to report, a bit of shouting outside my window tonight. Yes, just now, nothing more. Yes, let's hope so. Thank you, officer. Yes, I'll let you know. Goodnight.

Elsie What did they say?

John Nothing.

Elsie They must have said something.

John They said thank you for letting us know.

Elsie There you go, then.

Josh sits down at his computer again. The shouts subside. John takes Elsie's tray into the kitchen. He leaves it on the side. In BEDROOM TWO *Brian clutches his heart – a sharp spasm of pain at the same time as Elsie makes a similar gesture.*

That egg stuck in my gullet. I don't feel right.

SCENE FOUR

In BEDROOM ONE, *Louisa and the baby have fallen asleep. John leaves the kitchen and goes back to the* LOUNGE *and switches the TV on. He watches the news – the same news that Brian is watching.*

Elsie What do we want that on for?

John The news.

Elsie I want the other side. Five celebrities go to prison.

John It's the news!

Elsie I don't want this. I want the real-life programme. They're putting the weather girl in solitary confinement tonight.

John I just want to see this . . . This man murdered his family.

Elsie (*interested*) Did he?

Pause.

Barnaby leaves the BATHROOM *and goes into the* KITCHEN. *He looks at the tray that John has just left there – he clears the remains away. The magnifying glass goes into the drawer. Then he looks in the fridge. Sees Brian's half-eaten sandwich from earlier. Takes it out, sits miserably eating it.*

Brian watching the news on TV in BEDROOM TWO. *Janet enters.*

Brian That sandwich has given me heartburn.

Janet (*attention on the news*) Perhaps you're having a heart attack.

Pause. Brian frowns, but does not respond.

There's something good on the other side.

Brian They can't find a motive. They say it was totally motiveless.

John No signs of any struggling.

Elsie I wouldn't have slept through him murdering me. I'd have put up a fight.

Brian I reckon he drugged them first.

John He must have been mad.

Janet Oh no!

Elsie More than mad.

Brian He must have just snapped!

John Psychotic.

Janet Oh dear.

Elsie No death too good for him.

John Why did he do it?

Janet There must be a reason. Surely.

Brian He must have lived with the possibility of it. The thought of it in his head. Planned it, even. Planned it meticulously. Without thinking that he'd do it, maybe. But that night, he just went into another realm.

Elsie Ttt-ttt. Wickedness.

Janet Don't be morbid, Brian.

She gathers up her dressing gown, stays a moment, caught by the news.

Elsie Evil through and through.

Janet I think I'll have a shower. Relax me. (*sotto voce*) Oh dear.

From the darkness of BEDROOM ONE *we hear the sound of the baby crying. Extended crying. Barnaby sits eating his sandwich, listening. Seeing if Louisa will deal with it.*

Barnaby (*sotto voce*) Oh dear.

In BEDROOM TWO *Janet and Brian stop what they are doing, listen.*

Brian Here we go.

Janet I never let mine cry like that.

In the LOUNGE.

Elsie Listen to that.

John What?

Elsie Turn the tele down.

John does so. Elsie listens to the crying baby.

Ttt-ttt.

John It's just a baby. All babies cry.

Elsie I'm alert to the crying. It comes of being a telephonist for the emergency services. You can tell from the way people cry – whether it's a real emergency or not. Whether someone is in peril.

John Nobody's in peril, Mother.

Elsie People shake babies for less than that. Just a little shake and their brains spill out like pomegranates. It's a medical fact. Did you read about that woman? She had three – they all died before they were ten weeks. Unnatural.

SCENE FIVE

Barnaby enters BEDROOM ONE. *He picks the child up, takes her to Louisa, who is still lying down.*

Barnaby (*gently*) Don't let her cry. I thought we'd agreed not to let her cry! Louisa, wake up: she's crying, she's hungry.

Louisa I'm awake. I'm awake. Christ.

He puts the child in Louisa's arms.

Barnaby It's all right, baby girl, your milk is coming.

Louisa Not that side. I'm still sore that side.

Barnaby Sorry.

He turns the child round. Louisa starts to breast-feed the child. The child stops crying. Barnaby sits beside her, watches.

Elsie She's stopped.

Janet Must be feeding her.

Barnaby She's hungry.

Brian That or they've smothered her.

Janet Oh dear.

Louisa She's always hungry.

Janet I don't like the look of her. Thinks she's someone else.

Barnaby I don't think she's latched on properly.

Janet He looks all right.

Louisa You do it if you're such a bloody expert.

Janet Bit simple.

Barnaby I'm only trying to help.

Janet and Brian continue to listen. John turns up the tele again.

Elsie (*protests*) John!

John It's the headlines!

Barnaby and Louisa. Low hum of a news report in the back.

Barnaby You feel like a boxer. Coming round from a knockout punch. You're trying to rouse yourself before the referee gets to ten.

Louisa Please don't try and articulate things, Barnaby. It makes it worse, much much worse. Where were you?

Barnaby Eating a sandwich. It's given me heartburn.

He clutches his heart – a spasm of pain.

Louisa You need to relax. What time is it?

Barnaby It's . . . (*actual time*). I don't think you should have taken that pill. You find it too difficult to wake up.

Pause.

Louisa I dreamed that I lost the baby. Not this baby. But I knew that he was buried in the earth – but really low down – about one hundred feet down and I knew that if I worked hard enough I could get to him in time. So I started to bury down and at first I had an ice-cream scoop that I was using. And it was all really slow going, you know. And then the ice-cream scoop turned into a melon baller and that was even worse. So I threw it away and I was just doing it with my hands and sharp bits kept getting into my nails and my hands were cut to ribbons, but I could just hear the baby crying in the distance. But I knew that I'd never reach him. I just knew.

Barnaby (*softly*) But she's here.

Louisa (*curt*) Yep.

Barnaby Why don't you go and talk to someone?

Louisa When can I talk to someone? I have to feed her every five minutes.

Barnaby I'll take you.

Louisa I can't walk. I can't go anywhere for six weeks, that's what they said. Not until my scar's healed. Anyway, what about you? When are you going to sleep? If anyone's going to have a breakdown, it'll be you.

Barnaby Why do you see this as a competition?

Louisa You're driving me mad! With this endless vigil! You're such a bloody martyr!

The baby starts to cry.

Barnaby You've upset her now. She's crying.

Louisa It's always my fault. Take her, go on, take her. She's better off with you.

Barnaby She's hungry.

Louisa I can't do it. I can't do it. Just take her. Go on.

Barnaby takes her, tries to comfort her.

Elsie Raised voices.

Janet They're having a row!

Barnaby Don't say that.

Elsie They better not hurt that little one.

Louisa Well, it's true. We all know it's true.

Elsie They thrash them and blame it on the rain.

John (*with distaste*) Don't think like that.

Barnaby You've got to make a choice, Louisa. You either give in to this –

Louisa Yes, well, I give in! I give in!

Janet Brian, listen! Oh dear. Should we do something?

Elsie They microwaved one baby.

John That was a cat.

Elsie Same difference.

Janet Shall we call the police?

Brian They won't do anything.

Janet You never agree with me.

Brian What?

Janet Everything I say, you've always got an answer.

Shouts outside.

Elsie They're starting again! John!

Janet What's that now? More shouting!

John Ignore it!

Brian It's just kids. Why don't you relax?

Janet You know why.

Elsie I don't know how you can sit through it.

Janet I've got cancer.

John There's not a chance of that with you drawing my attention to it every five minutes.

Brian You haven't got cancer.

Janet You see! You see! This is what I'm talking about!

Brian sighs heavily.

Barnaby What's all that shouting in the street? We're trying to get a baby to sleep in here! Shut up, will you? Shut the fuck up, you morons!

John I don't know what's worse. Them hurling abuse at me. Or you drawing my attention to it every five minutes.

Elsie (*shouts*) Leave us alone! Mind your own business!

John Just grant me three wishes, would you?

Louisa (*crying*) Shut up! Shut up! Shut up!

Elsie Why don't you care, son?

Janet (*crying*) You don't care about me.

Louisa You're not helping! Stop it! You're not helping!

Janet (*crying*) I could be dying of cancer and you wouldn't care.

At the same time –

Brian Why are you crying?

Barnaby Why are you crying?

John Why are you crying?

At the same time –

Louisa Why do you think I'm crying?

Elsie Why do you think I'm crying?

Janet Why do you think I'm crying?

At the same time –

Brian I can't take much more of this.

John I can't take much more of this.

Barnaby I can't take much more of this.

Louisa (in BEDROOM ONE*) and Elsie (in the* LOUNGE*) and Janet (in* BEDROOM TWO*) cry. John storms out, goes to the* KITCHEN*, breathing, trying to control himself. The baby cries quietly. Barnaby tries to comfort the baby, walks out of the room, paces back and forth in the* HALLWAY*.*

Shsh. Shsh. There there, little one.

There are intermittent cries in the street. Janet exits and takes a shower with her back to the audience. She feels for lumps under her arms. Brian takes his hammer out, nurses it like a baby, at the same time as Barnaby.

Brian There, there, little one.

At the same time, John picks up the kitchen knife. Louisa stares blankly ahead.

At the same time –

I have bad thoughts.

John I have bad thoughts.

Louisa I have bad thoughts.

One after another –

Brian My own wife.

Louisa My own child.

John My own mother.

All of them are left with their thoughts.

SCENE SIX

In BEDROOM ONE.

Barnaby You talk to me. Talk to Daddy. Tell me what's wrong. Eh?

The baby cries. He puts her very gently back into the Moses basket, watches over her. He hums/la-las very softly, tries to soothe her.

At the same time as he rocks her and hums, the light in the STUDY *reaches an intensity. Josh types on his computer. He speaks for the first time.*

Josh You want to talk to me? Yeah. Why not? You can be my buddy for the night. Hello, buddy! What shall I call you. Daddy? That's original. Okay, Daddy, smiley-face, I want 2 chat. I always want to chat! That's me. U can call me . . . um . . . Babycakes. Enter. Sticking-tongue-out face. (*He stops typing.*) Stop crying, baby. Don't cry. Don't be frightened. They teach you that. That's what they do. From the moment you're born. FEAR, press SEND! It's all – don't do this, you can't do that, you can't, you just can't, all right? You're like wide open when you're born – just accepting it all, you know, and then they throw all this shit at you – and slowly they close you off. Then they start thinking bad thoughts about you. It's like they want you to fail. To go off the rails. They want to turn you into their worst fears. That's what they want. (*He types again.*) Ha, ha. LOL. Laughing out loud, buddy. Y not? What did u have in mind?

He stops. The baby cries still louder.

I used to be scared of the dark, baby. I thought there was something lurking in the corner – a man in the shadows who was going to hurt me. I used to shit myself. I'm not frightened any more. Because I surrendered to him . . . You know what I did? I invited him in. I talk to the man in the shadows. (*He reads the screen.*) Who are u, babycakes? (*He types again.*) I am whoever u want me to b. Winking-smiley-face.

He stops. The baby is gradually stopping crying.

There, you see, it's not so bad, is it? You can be nocturnal like me! It's when everything expands. You can start testing the limits. (*He reads.*) What do I do? What do I do? (*He types.*) I peddle terror. Yelling-face.

> *He gets up – puts his music on – Eminem rallying-type music. In the next house Barnaby reacts with exasperation, bangs on a wall.*

Barnaby Turn it down! Turn it down!

> *Josh turns the music up.*

Josh He likes it, don't you, babycakes? (*He types.*) I peddle terror. Yeah. I'm a virus. Exclamation mark. (*He reads.*) Y? (*He types.*) Because I can. Because I found out I can. Yelling-face. Ha ha. TTFN. (*He stops. Gets up.*) Ta-ta for now.

> *In the* STUDY, *he goes to a drawer. Takes out a balaclava.*

Barnaby (*in exasperation*) What is happening tonight, please? Will somebody tell me? What is happening?

> *Josh puts the balaclava on.*

> *In the* BATHROOM.

Janet (*in the shower, strangely calm, a litany*) I am dying. I am dying. I am dying.

> *In* BEDROOM TWO.

Brian (*holding the hammer*) One blow to the head. All it takes. And there'd be an end to it.

> *In* BEDROOM ONE.

Louisa (*in the bed*) I am not a mother. There's been a terrible mistake. I am not a mother. I am not a mother.

> *In the* KITCHEN, *John shouts out into the darkness.*

John I am not a paedophile. Do you hear me? I am not a paedophile. I am not a paedophile.

In the LOUNGE *Elsie starts to drop off, sitting up.*

Josh climbs out of the window of his STUDY.

SCENE SEVEN

The power cuts out. Janet's shower stops. Both TVs cut out. The lights go out. There is silence and complete darkness. They all speak at once, but softly.

Louisa Oh my God!

Brian Oh shit! What the –

Janet Ahh!

John Oh no. What now?

Barnaby Christ!

Then slowly they talk their way out of the darkness. Softly, starting to overlap, it should sound almost like a prayer.

Janet Brian?

Barnaby Louisa?

Brian Jan?

Louisa I'm here.

Janet I'm all wet –

Brian I can't see –

John A thing.

Janet My dressing gown. Where's my –?

Barnaby Are you –

Louisa I'm all right. Is the baby –

Janet Where's my dressing gown?

John Mother?

Barnaby I think she's –

John Asleep.

Barnaby (*laughs*) She's asleep.

Louisa A power cut.

Brian Must be –

John It's a power cut.

Janet A power cut.

Brian A pissing power cut.

Barnaby Where's the fuse box? Maybe it's just a trip switch.

Louisa No, look, the lights are off outside.

Pause. All the characters look out.

Janet, Brian, Barnaby and Louise repeat the same lines one after another in the form of a round:

Janet No street lights.
The whole streer.
No one has power.
The grid must be down.

Brian, John, Barnaby and Louisa repeat the round. This spurs them all to start walking. They should bump into each other in the dark, as if they were bumping into furniture. John gropes his way up to BEDROOM ONE *and then down again to the* LOUNGE *to see his mother.*

Barnaby starts to make his way to the LOUNGE. *Janet is heading for the* KITCHEN. *Brian goes into the* LOUNGE *and then back into the* KITCHEN.

Janet Brian, the power's gone off!

Brian The whole street's out.

Barnaby I'll go and see if I can find some candles.

John Mother?

Janet I think there's some candles in here. You'd better go and check on Josh.

Brian Why?

Janet He'll be in the dark.

Brian Oh yes.

Louisa Give her to me –

Barnaby Are you sure –

Louisa Quickly. It's cold. She's probably hungry.

John Mother?

Janet He's scared of the dark. And he hasn't had his pudding yet.

Brian Is he?

Janet I used to leave a night light out for him. Remember?

John Are you all right?

Barnaby You'll be all right?

Louisa No, all manner of ill will befall us.

Barnaby What?

Janet We don't know what's happened to him.

Brian The computer will have stopped!

Janet He might talk to you. What are you waiting for?

Louisa Go on, go. We will be fine. We will prosper.

Brian I'll go and see, then.

Barnaby If you're sure you're all right. You won't –

Janet Get a move on. He might have lost files and things. His dot-coms. He might be upset.

Brian hesitates – is he a little scared of his son?

Brian Why don't you go?

Janet I took him his dinner.

Brian I don't want to go.

Janet Someone should check on him.

Brian Right. Yes. I'll see if I've got a torch for him first. I might have one upstairs.

Brian goes and looks for a torch in BEDROOM TWO.

Janet Go on then, quickly. What's wrong with you?

Barnaby hands Louisa the baby.

Barnaby Don't upset her, careful. You're shaking her!

Louisa I'm not shaking her – Barnaby! Go on, for Christ's sake.

John enters the LOUNGE. *He is shaking his mother.*

John Mother? Mother?

Barnaby goes to the BATHROOM. *Janet sees that Brian has exited without the pudding. She takes a spoon out and starts eating some of the crème brûlée. Brian is looking in* BEDROOM TWO. *He gets out his hammer. Takes it downstairs.*

SCENE EIGHT

In the LOUNGE.

John Mother? Mother? Christ. You can't be dead, not in the middle of a bloody power cut. That'd be just like you.

Pause, he stops shaking her. Everyone in all the cells breaks off for a moment, listens.

(*quietly*) My mother may at last at this moment be dead.

Elsie wakes up with a jolt.

Elsie Emergency service! Which service do you require?

Activity resumes.

John Mother?

Elsie Ambulance? Fire or Police?

John There's been a power cut.

Elsie A what?

John The heating's gone off. Do you want me to help you into bed?

Elsie No, I do not. Get your dirty hands off me.

John I'm not touching you. (*He goes to go.*)

Elsie Where are you going? You can't leave me here in the dark.

John Close your eyes. Imagine it's not there.

Elsie Talk to me. John! Tell me a story.

John What are you talking about?

Elsie A story to chase the night away. Go on.

John You're getting confused again.

Elsie My marbles are quite intact, thank you very much. I want a story.

John There once was a wicked old woman who told terrrible lies so they sewed up her mouth and all the bad thoughts spewed out of her eyes and her nose and her ears and her arsehole. The effort of not speaking rubbish quite killed her. She died horribly and alone. The end. The end. The end.

Elsie I'm not alone.

John No. No, you're not.

Elsie (*a cackle – she has caught him out*) Ha! Ha!

John I'll get a torch.

John goes to go. Pause.

Elsie Stay with me, John.

John I'm only going upstairs.

Barnaby goes back to BEDROOM ONE. *John exits, goes to* BEDROOM TWO. *He looks for a torch.*

Barnaby I couldn't find anything.

Louisa I don't think we've got any.

Barnaby I think I should go next door. Shall I go next door?

Elsie Don't leave me, John.

Barnaby They might have candles. The baby'll get cold. Is she warm enough?

Louisa I don't know. You feel.

Elsie I'm cold.

Barnaby I shouldn't leave you two, should I?

Louisa That's a decision only you can make.

Barnaby I think I'll go next door. I think that's what I should do. Yes. Definitely. Will you be okay?

Louisa It'll probably come back on in a minute.

Barnaby But in case it doesn't? You'll be all right? I won't be long. You'll watch over her?

Brian Josh?

Elsie John?

Louisa Of course I'll watch her. What else am I going to do?

Elsie I'm having bad thoughts.

Brian stands before the STUDY. *He's holding his hammer.*

Brian Josh?

At the same time, Janet searches for and eventually finds candles.

Barnaby Baby?

Brian Are you all right, son? It's me – your dad. The power's gone –

Barnaby The power's gone and I'm going to sort things out.

Brian I'm sure it'll get sorted.

Barnaby Back in a twinkling.

Brian Won't be long.

Barnaby You sleep and dream of angels.

Brian Josh? Are you asleep? You wouldn't tell me, would you, even if you were? You wouldn't tell me, just to spite me. You could be – dead. You could be cold as stone and you wouldn't tell me, would you?

Brian puts his head in his hands – suddenly overwhelmed with sadness. A small vigil. Barnaby hands the baby back to Louisa during the next.

Louisa Just go. Before you turn to bloody stone. Why don't you – you're driving me mad – just go – I can't breathe with you in here – bloody well go!

Barnaby leaves.

Brian Josh?

Elsie Can you hear me?

Brian (*quietly*) It's your mother you want, isn't it? A boy always wants his mother.

In the LOUNGE.

Elsie Your dad saw a ghost the moment before he died. That moment between alive and dead. He looked up and he called out 'Mother'. And not a word of a lie, it was like the years just dropped off his face. Like he was a boy again. I didn't recognise him.

Silence. Then Louisa switches on the battery-operated baby-monitor light.

Louisa There. All the better to see you with.

SCENE NINE

The front doorbell goes.

Brian Doorbell.

Louisa We can't get it, can we?

Brian Janet?

Elsie John?

John (*reacting to the doorbell*) Oh, piss off and leave me alone, why don't you?

Janet (*to herself*) I'm not getting it. It could be anyone.

Louisa They'll go away.

Brian goes to the window. Elsie, alone in the dark.

Elsie My mother used to tell me ghost stories in the dark. I wet myself once. This dark puddle on the floor, when the lights went on. She was so cross, she nearly killed me.

In BEDROOM ONE *Louisa speaks to the baby. In the* KITCHEN *Janet starts to light candles. In* BEDROOM TWO, *John gives up his search for a torch. He cradles his broken arm and then lies down on the bed, suddenly weary from all his exertions.*

Louisa (*to the bundle*) Are you wet? Oh dear. Wet through. I can't do anything about that at the moment. I'm afraid I'm not able to meet your needs . . . Do you like me? Do you? I used to be different. I used to . . . once upon a time I was a singer. In Italy, they called me 'Principessa' and one man said he would sell his soul to hear me sing. But that's not important – the important thing is me and your daddy – we went travelling through the whole wide world and we laughed and we thought we'd have a basketful of children and so we bought this shoe and we thought we would be happy . . . But something happened to us, I can't really – and my throat closed over and we thought that you would make us all better. We made a mistake. We rushed into it. And now we don't laugh. We just wait for you to cry . . . What are you thinking? You have no words, but do you still think? Do you think wordless thoughts? I do. Thoughts that shouldn't have words, thoughts that shy away from the words. I think . . . you're so tiny, with that silly floppy head. I think . . . you don't look like a person yet. I think

I could gobble you up . . . I could . . . tear you limb from limb. It's better to say these things, isn't it? If you say them – the thoughts evaporate – the birds catch them in the air and scatter them far away from you . . . Don't they? The bad thoughts . . . Thinking it doesn't count. But sometimes I do think, baby. I think it would be easier without you. Not to live through all the minutes and hours and days and months, willing you to live. Is she all right? Is she still all right? He's trying to watch you every minute, your daddy. But at some point he'll fail. He'll turn away and that'll be it. Won't it? You won't be all right and he will have failed and that'll be an end to it.

The dooorbell rings again. Brian answers it.

SCENE TEN

Elsie sits and broods in the LOUNGE.

In the KITCHEN *Janet has lit the candles. She stands a little awed by the atmosphere. At the door:*

Barnaby I'm from next door. I'm sorry.

Brian I thought you'd gone away.

Barnaby No. I'm from next door. I wondered if you had candles?

Pause.

Brian (*indicating the interior of the house*) Janet.

Brian goes towards the KITCHEN. *Barnaby hestitates and then follows him. Brian enters. Janet jumps.*

Janet You scared me half to death. Is he all right? Josh?

Brian Early night.

Barnaby enters the KITCHEN.

Janet Bless him.

Brian We've got a visitor!

Janet Oh my goodness, do excuse me, I look like a witch – wet hair!

Barnaby (*awkward*) Umm. I'm terribly sorry to bother you. It's just we've only just moved, you know.

Janet Yes. I know. We saw you – the day you – we said 'professional people', didn't we, Brian?

Brian Yes.

Janet What is it that you do, then?

Barnaby Urm – I'm an architect. And then we've just had the baby –

Brian An architect?

Barnaby We might have candles, but God knows where they are. And I was just worried about the cold, you know – with the baby, when they're new-born you have to keep them constant. Their skin is still so thin –

Janet Next to nothing. You can see the veins pulsing, can't you?

Janet suddenly notices the hammer in Brian's hand.

Brian!

Brian What?

Janet The hammer! What a welcome to our new neighbour.

Brian Oh, sorry.

Janet Give it to me. He keeps it under the bed, in case someone tries to murder him. Who'd murder him, I say? Who'd bother, eh?

Brian What do you mean?

Janet (*laughs*) Nobody'd murder you.

Brian What do you mean?

Janet Someone's got to want to murder you.

Brian They murder you for your mobile phone these days.

Janet You can't work your mobile phone.

Brian It's not about stealing things any more. They murder you if you're in the way. Just if you happen to be in the way. They just want to invade your private space. They want to crush you. That's what they want.

Janet You see! Always with the answer! Sit down, sit down, Mr –

Barnaby Barnaby.

Janet Janet. Brian! (*indicating the hammer*) Give it to me. What? (*Janet puts the hammer away in a drawer.*) Brian, give Barnaby a drink.

Barnaby I just wanted to get some candles and maybe –

Janet You'll have to excuse me, Barnaby, I was just in the shower, you know, when the power went. I'm dripping wet. You must think I look like a witch.

Barnaby Really it was just to see if you had any spare candles – and maybe a propane-gas heater.

Janet A propane-gas heater?

Brian A propane-gas heater?

Barnaby We haven't got any form of heat.

Janet Brian'll go and look.

Brian There might be something in the shed.

Janet Yes! Sit down, Barnaby, you look very tired. It's exhausting, isn't it, the first few weeks? We saw the little bundle coming home! Boy or girl?

Barnaby Girl.

Janet We've got a boy. Fourteen, he is. A big boy now.

Barnaby What's his name?

Josh enters the house, near BEDROOM ONE *– the sense that he has broken in, through a window. He lurks in the shadows.*

At the same time, eager:

Janet Josh!

Brian Josh!

Janet What's her name? Your little one.

Barnaby She hasn't got a name. I mean, you don't have to, legally, till they're six weeks old and we just haven't, you know . . .

Janet Oh dear. (*long drawn-out – woes of the world*) Oh dear! What a shame. Why not?

Brian (*admonishing*) Janet! So what if the baby hasn't got a name? You'll have to excuse my wife.

Janet What do you mean?

Brian You never stop, do you?

Janet I wasn't criticising.

Brian Janet is one of those people who constantly feels sorry for other people.

Janet I'm sensitive!

Brian She'll only buy a magazine if it's got a headless baby on the cover. She loves it.

Janet I do not.

Brian If she could give herself cancer pretending to worry about other people she would.

Janet I'm not pretending.

Brian That's the latest. She thinks she's got cancer. She's been to the doctor's about it. Nothing wrong with her. Bleedin' Munchausen's-by-proxy—bleeding mad she is.

Janet Barnaby, you feel under here, what's that if it isn't a growth?

Brian Janet! He's an architect!

Barnaby I really should get back –

Brian That's right. Don't encourage her. It's all in her head.

Janet I can't help it if the world is full of tragedy.

Brian You've never even come close to tragedy. What do you know about it?

Janet Oh here we go – I know this routine. How tragedy touched my sad little life, by Brian Wheeler.

Brian Well, let's let Barney be the judge of that – Barney, Barney, I've got a story for you here. A scary story. Are you listening?

Barnaby Yes, yes –

Brian I'm a lorry driver, long-distance. I'm not now – I'm on the sick, but I used to be so – you know – up in my little cabin, music, driving all over the land. Far and wide – on my own. A friendly chat here and there. Tales from the road, you know the sort of thing, innocent. Then, wham, one day I have a blackout. Out of the blue. No recollection of it whatsoever. Like a sledgehammer through my brain. All the wiring went. They say you can be programmed to have it from the minute you're born. Upshot was, I lost control. Careered off the motorway – through the crash-barrier, down the embankment. Do you know where I ended up?

Janet Right by a railway line.

Brian (*rattled*) I'm telling this. This is my story. Do you know what time it was? Four o'clock in the afternoon – it was the school train I would have hit.

Janet But you didn't hit it.

Brian Inches away from a major catastrophe.

Janet But it didn't happen.

Brian Just like that other bloke. He's in prison now.

Janet But you're not.

Brian I can't drive now. I have flashbacks.

Janet How can you have flashbacks if you don't remember it?

Brian When something like that happens to you, you can't go back. Brain overload, that's what I've got. She's never come close to that feeling.

Janet I have. Every night with you.

Barnaby Sorry, do you think you have a torch or anything? I can't leave them –

Janet Oh yes! Do excuse us, we're not used to company. Well, I'll pop upstairs again. See if there's any more where these came from.

Janet exits with a candle and goes to BEDROOM TWO. *As she does she passes John who goes into the* BATHROOM. *He stands under the waterless shower. Janet does not look for candles. She puts her candle down and sits on the bed and looks at herself as if into a mirror. After a while she starts to preen herself, doll herself up, perhaps apply lipstick in the dark.*

There is a lull in the conversation in the KITCHEN. *Brian fixes Barnaby a drink.*

SCENE ELEVEN

Josh enters BEDROOM ONE *behind Louisa. Louisa does not see him. Louisa talks to the baby.*

Louisa It's weird when you do that. When you look beyond me like that. Who are you looking at? Who can you see?

Janet Mirror, mirror, on the wall . . .

Louisa puts the baby in the Moses basket with some difficulty. She has a lot of difficulty moving because of her Caesarean scar. She winces with pain.

Louisa I need to rest now. The pill's making Mummy's head fuzzy. Where has your daddy got to?

Josh does not make a sound.

(*drowsily*) Is it an angel? Is that it? Can you see an angel?

Josh looks at Louisa and then he looks at the Moses basket. He stands very still.

In the KITCHEN.

Barnaby I think I should be getting back.

Brian hands him a drink.

Brian Whisky.

Barnaby It's very cold, isn't it?

Brian There'll be people die tonight, you mark my words. Old folk . . . and the like. The weak and the vulnerable.

Barnaby I hope not. Thank you. I need this. (*He takes a sip. Sighs.*) A sudden wave of tiredness.

John sinks down under the shower. Elsie sighs. Louisa turns over in bed. Janet lifts up the bags under her eyes.

A little break. Perhaps I just need a little break.

Brian I'll go and look in the shed. Out into the wilderness!

Brian exits. John gets up and goes back into the LOUNGE. *Barnaby is on his own. He speaks into the darkness.*

In BEDROOM ONE, *Josh kneels down before the Moses basket. He looks closely – an echo of what Barnaby did earlier when checking her breathing.*

Barnaby We cannot name her because we are scared. Because our first baby died, you see. A cot death. At seventeen weeks. For no apparent reason. And now we are living in fear and we cannot commit our hearts to this child in case she dies too. That is why.

Barnaby drinks. During the next, his mood sinks very low.

SCENE TWELVE

LOUNGE. *Darkness (just the spillover of improvised light/ candles from other rooms). Elsie sits. John re-enters.*

John I couldn't find anything.

Elsie (*whisper*) You like men, don't you?

John What?

Elsie (*normal voice*) Men? You like them? Don't you?

John I heard you the first time.

Elsie You've never had the good grace to tell me.

John Where's all this come from all of a sudden?

Elsie You should've told me.

John It's none of your business.

Elsie How can you say that? When you're living under my roof. When bricks get thrown through my window. When I have to watch it all?

John (*mumble*) That's got nothing to do with –

Elsie Speak up, don't mumble.

John It doesn't concern you.

Elsie I'm not saying I don't find it disgusting. But I have a right to know.

John Why?

Elsie Because sometimes I am scared of you. The not knowing, the unknowing, makes me frightened of you.

John sits but is silent. Elsie waits.

In BEDROOM ONE, *Josh picks the baby up. Louisa sleeps. Her sleep is unsettled.*

Josh (*softly, gently*) You're not frightened, are you? Not frightened of me? You know no fear, do you? None at all.

He looks at the baby. Barnaby in the KITCHEN *gets up.*

Barnaby Janet!

In BEDROOM TWO.

Janet I'm here! Come and find me!

Josh Shsh. Mummy's sleeping. We don't want to wake her up.

Barnaby walks to BEDROOM TWO.

In the LOUNGE.

John (*with difficulty*) I like men.

Elsie Why?

John What do you mean, why?

Elsie There must be a reason.

John Some things are for no reason.

Elsie When did it happen?

John It didn't happen. It's who I am.

Josh You don't know who you are yet, do you? You're a little in-between.

Barnaby enters BEDROOM TWO.

Janet Come and sit beside me.

Elsie Do you have sex in parks?

John does not answer.

Barnaby Have you found any candles?

Janet I prefer it in the dark.

Josh We like the dark, don't we, babycakes?

Elsie That's what they do, isn't it? They go looking for it, all furtive looks in the greenery.

In BEDROOM ONE *Louisa, who is still asleep, sits up – and starts to burrow down into the sheets. At the same time Barnaby sits down in* BEDROOM TWO.

John You don't know anything about it.

Janet I get very pent up. I want to be released from my head. Do you know that feeling, Barnaby?

Elsie Well, do you?

Barnaby Yes. My wife – we – since all this –

Louisa I can't get to him. Barnaby!

Janet You need to relax. Let me take care of you. (*She starts to massage his shoulders.*)

Josh Look at Mummy. Silly Mummy.

Josh rocks the baby and hums strangely.

Barnaby I should go.

Elsie Have you ever?

John I'm not answering that.

Janet You don't have to do anything. I will put a spell on you. Close your mind. Shsh.

Josh Babycakes, babycakes, poor little babycakes.

Elsie Are you careful?

John Yes. Stop asking me this.

Janet Surrender to it.

Louisa's bad dream worsens, her movements are frantic. Barnaby closes his eyes.

Elsie You must do it down alleyways and the like, because you don't do it here. I'd know if you did.

John (*angry*) I don't do it at all, all right! Not for a long time. I don't do it at all. And even if I did it would be nothing to do with you.

Louisa I can't get to him. Barnaby?

Barnaby I am very tired. All the effort.

Janet Let me breathe for you.

Barnaby What?

Josh You have to surrender to it.

Janet I will breathe for you.

They kiss. Barnaby has surrendered to it.

SCENE THIRTEEN

In BEDROOM ONE *Louisa is waking groggily.*

Louisa My hands – Barnaby – you've got to help me.

Elsie I'm glad your father never knew. He'd have never lived it down, what with being in the fire service. He'd never have got over it.

John Shut up! Shut up! Be quiet. I'm not talking any more. There's an end to it.

Louisa I'll never ever get to him in time.

Elsie and John sit in the darkness.

Janet It will be like it never happened.

Elsie There's a torch in the dining room. In the cupboard.

John gets up goes to the DINING ROOM/STUDY. *During the next scene he finds the torch, checks it works and then sits down, tired suddenly. He sits at the computer.*

In BEDROOM ONE *Louisa sees Josh. She is still groggy. During the next Barnaby and Janet proceed to have sex.*

Louisa (*innocent, sleepy*) Have you come to take her away?

Josh Hello, Mummy.

John They call me names and they try to turn me into something that I am not. They try to make me think their way. They try to infect me. I don't want to think these things. I don't want to sin even in thought.

Josh You've been having a nightmare.

Louisa comes to.

Louisa Oh my God!

Josh Don't scream. Whatever you do – don't scream.

Louisa Please – please – give me the baby – please –

Josh Shsh.

Louisa tries to be quiet, calm.

Louisa I'm not strong at the moment. I've just had a baby. I can't move. Please. If you want money, there's some downstairs. My bag is in the kitchen. Take it. Take the video. We've got a DVD. My mobile phone. Anything. What is it you want?

Josh Why do you think I want something from you?

Louisa Give the baby to me.

Josh I'm just holding her.

Louisa You can hurt me but don't touch her.

Josh What makes you think I'm going to hurt her?

Louisa My husband's next door. He'll be back any minute.

Small murmurs from Janet and Barnaby.

Josh She's so light. So small. Fragile.

Louisa No, she's not. She's strong. She's surprisingly strong.

Josh Ha! She's smiling at me.

Louisa She's not smiling. She's too little to smile.

Josh Yeah, that's right . . . She has to learn to smile. She has to find something to smile about, doesn't she? What if she doesn't? What if she never learns to smile?

Louisa She'll smile at me. I will smile at her and she'll learn.

Brian enters the KITCHEN *– he holds a Calor gas heater in his hand. He is smiling, happy.*

Brian Janet?

He makes his way up to BEDROOM TWO.

Josh How can you bring her into this world? How?

Louisa Put the baby down.

Josh This terrible world. Poor baby.

Louisa She will be all right, because we will love her. We will try to be the best parents that we can be to her. We will try our best to keep her from harm.

Josh That's what they all say.

Louisa tries to get up.

Don't get up. I could hurt her. I could shake her. I could throw her against that wall.

Louisa No, please, please.

Josh She needs to learn about it. She needs to learn there's so much evil out there. Do you believe in evil?

John I am a good man.

Louisa I don't know. Please. My husband is just – he went next door.

Brian enters BEDROOM TWO. *He stands a moment, watching Barnaby and Janet having sex. Perhaps Janet sees him but Barnaby does not. Brian's face is impassive. Barnaby is coming to a climax.*

Josh Man the other day raped a fifteen-month-old baby. Took pictures of himself while he was doing it.

John is sitting at the computer in the STUDY. *Louisa starts to cry.*

John These are my worst thoughts. Thoughts of young boys. Boys of fourteen, fifteen. I send them into the net. I scatter them into the world. There's no power tonight. It's safe. What I think – what I write – will disappear. Nobody will see my thoughts, nobody will read them. So they will evaporate. Yes.

He starts to type on the keyboard.

Louisa (*crying*) If you want to have sex, have sex with me. Just put her down, please.

Josh I chat with them all the time. On the net. You can't shield her from that.

John continues to type.

Louisa I will do my best.

Josh Your best will never be good enough. The minute she learns to smile she becomes a victim.

Pause. Barnaby comes. Janet does not. Brian leaves without saying anything. Neither of them see him. He walks to the KITCHEN.

Louisa He must be coming back. That's him. I can hear him. You'll have to go.

Josh That's not him.

Louisa No, it's him, he's coming back.

Josh Perhaps he's left you? Perhaps he's gone for good. Have you considered that?

Pause. John finishes typing. Sits back, purged. Brian goes into the KITCHEN. *He looks in a kitchen drawer. He stands staring at it.*

In BEDROOM TWO, *Barnaby and Janet lie side by side on the bed.*

Josh Are you scared?

Louisa The lights will come back on . . . and my husband will come back.

Josh Are you scared of me?

Louisa I am scared of what you will do to her.

Josh You're scared of me. Just say it.

Louisa I'm scared of you.

Josh That's all I wanted to know. Here you go. (*He kisses the baby on the head. He hands her the baby.*) She's sweet. There you see. No harm done. I haven't hurt you, have I?

Louisa No.

Josh I haven't hurt her.

Louisa No.

John stops typing.

John No harm done.

Josh Good. I'm going now. You will stay here, for ten minutes. You will sit tight with her. Until I have gone, okay?

Louisa Okay. Yes.

Josh That's it – get under the covers with her. Stay in the dark with her. Lie down. Surrender to it. Yes?

Louisa Yes. Thank you.

Josh It'll be as if none of this ever happened.

SCENE FOURTEEN

Josh exits the house. Louisa cries softly under the covers. In the KITCHEN *Brian sees the half-eaten crème brûlée. He takes out a spoon, and during the next he eats it.*

Barnaby I love my wife. I hope you know that.

Janet Yes.

Louisa (*quietly*) Barnaby?

In BEDROOM ONE *Louisa gets up with difficulty – puts the baby into a sling and goes into the* BATHROOM. *All her movements are very laboured, because of her Caesarean wound. She washes her face.*

Barnaby I fell in love with her at first sight. She was singing on stage. It was like coming up from the deepest, darkest well. I thought, if I cannot have her, I will die. She makes me want to build glass domes. Glass domes that will shatter at the purity of her voice. She will sing and the glass will shatter and I will build her another dome. I will never stop building domes for her to sing in.

Janet Yes.

Barnaby I was not myself tonight. I was tired and confused. I wasn't feeling right. I'm very, very sorry.

Janet Yes.

Barnaby I need to walk. I need to breathe fresh air and then I need to return to my family as if none of this had happened.

Janet Yes.

Barnaby gets up and exits. Brian finishes eating the crème brûlée. He goes to the STUDY.

Brian Josh? Are you listening? I'm sick of it. I'm sick of being inches away from a catastrophe. For years I have been inches away. I would rather that it happened now. It would be much better if it just happened. I want to enter another realm.

He goes to go, turns back –

I'm afraid I've eaten your pud.

He goes back into the KITCHEN. *First of all he tidies up the kitchen, wipes it clean. At the same time John enters the* LOUNGE *with the torch.*

John I found the torch.

Elsie I'm sorry, John.

John It works. We've got light now.

Elsie We won't talk about it any more. That will be an end to it. It's as if none of it happened. I'm not saying it doesn't hurt me. The fact you've robbed me of my second chance. I have to hand out sweets to strangers now because of you. And lots of them won't take my sweets. Little bastards. They should be grateful . . . And all this palaver now – with the accusations, maybe none of that would have happened if you'd been a decent family man. But we won't say any more about it.

Louisa exits the house. Brian takes the hammer out of the drawer. Josh enters the house in the KITCHEN *as Brian leaves it to go to* BEDROOM TWO. *Josh looks in the same drawers for a weapon. He cannot find the hammer so he picks up the knife – considers it as a weapon, then discards it.*

John Being gay doesn't make you a paedophile.

Elsie There's no smoke without burning, son.

John Ninety per cent of paedophiles are straight.

Elsie How do you know so much about it?

John You think I do it, don't you? You think I have sex with children.

Elsie I'm not saying anything. But people draw conclusions. Single man lives with his mother, runs a video shop. What do you expect?

John You stupid ignorant old woman. You're my mother and you have no faith in me. No wonder I don't stand a chance. Sometimes I want to shake you – shake you till you see sense. You stupid old hag!

Brian enters BEDROOM TWO. *Janet gets up before he can reach her. She pushes past him. He grabs hold of her. At the same time, John takes hold of Elsie.*

(*murderous*) You don't realise how far you push me!

Brian You don't realise how far you push me!

Brian grabs Janet with one hand and raises the hammer to Janet. John grabs hold of his mother. At the same time:

Janet Let go of me!

Elsie Let go of me!

Janet Murder me, would you?

Elsie Murder me in the dark and make it look like –

Janet Make it look like – an accident?

Elsie – hypothermia?

Janet An overdose?

Elsie A trick of the light?

At the same time:

Janet You'll never get away with it!

Elsie You'll never get away with it!

Elsie They'll string you up.

Janet They'll hang you out to dry.

Brian Perhaps I don't want to get away with it.

John Perhaps that's what I want.

At the same time:

Elsie Go on then, if you're such a big man. Put me out of my misery. You'll be doing me a favour.

Janet Go on then, if you're such a big man. Put me out of my misery. You'll be doing me a favour.

The men let go. The women laugh.

Ha!

Elsie Ha!

John What's that?

Janet Get out of my way, Brian. If I'm going to die, I don't need your help, thank you very much.

Brian Where are you going?

Janet I can't breathe in here. I'm going outside.

She exits. Brian collapses on the bed, defeated.

Elsie That's what they do to old folk these days. Mug them and then pretend it's because they didn't have proper heating. You read about it every day in the newspaper.

John Shsh! Shsh! You stupid old woman. I can hear something. There's someone moving about in the house! Listen!

Brian slowly places the hammer back under the bed and lies down. Perhaps he cries. During the next he falls asleep. Josh's weapon of choice is a blowtorch (a kitchen one to make crème brûlée etc.). He takes it out of the drawer and lights it with a lighter in his pocket.

Elsie John!

Josh enters the LOUNGE *with the blowtorch.*

John! Oh my God! Emergency! He's got a gun.

John It's not a gun.

Elsie We are in peril! John! We are definitely in peril. Call the fire – ambulance – police!

Josh Tell her to get out. It's you I want to talk to.

Elsie He'll set us alight. We're all going to fry to a crisp.

John Mother, go upstairs.

Elsie I told you to change the batteries in the smoke alarm.

Josh Go on, old woman. Do as he says.

John Go on, Mother. Now. Everything will be all right. I'll sort this out. Go on.

Elsie Oh dear. This is it. This is it!

Elsie exits – she goes into BEDROOM TWO *and takes out the hammer from under the bed, then she goes and sits in* BEDROOM ONE *on the bed and pulls the covers around her. Josh goes up to John with the blowtorch. He threatens him with it.*

Josh Moths are drawn to the light.

John Okay. Let's just be calm now. Let's think this through.

Josh I know what they say about you.

John They tell lies about me.

Josh Do you want to have sex with me?

John I'm not a paedophile.

Josh That wasn't the question.

John How old are you?

Josh What age do you want me to be?

John You're only young.

Josh That's how you like them, isn't it?

John No.

Josh I can morph for you, John. We can test the limits together. I'm in-between, John. I'm a lovely in-between.

John I don't understand.

Josh Come on. You can be yourself now. You can drop the crap.

John I am being myself. I am trying to be myself.

Josh I won't tell anyone. When did you last have an offer like that, eh?

John I don't want to have sex with you.

Josh Nobody's looking.

John You don't know that.

Josh Guy the other day had sex with a fifteen-month-old. Turn you on, did it?

John I am going to call the police now.

Josh Only got five years. Not bad.

John Please stop. You can burn me if you like. I'm an easy target – my arm is broken, my face is beaten up, I won't put up much of a fight. If it will make you feel better, then do it. Come on.

Josh No, no, that's not what you want.

He switches off the blowtorch.

There, that's better. We're in the dark. That's where you like to be, isn't it? I understand that. That's where I like to be, too. Do you want me to talk about it first? Do you want to hear the words? What we could do together? Is that what you need first? Do you need the words to become thoughts before you can do anything?

John You're clever. You're very clever.

Josh Are you thinking about it? Like the idea, do you? Why not? I can see it in your face. It's okay. I know you can't help yourself.

John I'm not a paedophile.

Josh No.

John And you're not a child.

Josh That's right. Let's create our own version. Whatever makes you comfortable.

John You would go through with this?

Josh Why not?

John You would let me abuse you?

Josh It's not abuse if I want it too. If I surrender to it.

John But why?

Josh Sometimes there isn't a reason. That's the funny thing. Things just happen.

John I don't believe that.

Josh I want to feel things, John. I want to feel things, too.

John You poor boy.

Josh Let's do something then. What are you waiting for?

Pause. John moves up to him. He moves very close, within kissing distance.

John (*quietly, into his ear*) You think you can get inside my head. Make me live in fear. But I choose not to.

Josh What?

John I may not fit in my own skin but you will never turn me into that. You can't make me live by your rules. I choose not to. Every single time I choose not to.

Josh touches him provocatively

Josh You're scared of me, aren't you?

John Yes. And sometimes I am scared of myself. Which is worse. (*John sits quietly.*) I am very, very tired. If you want to know the truth, I am in despair. I am in a state of despair.

Josh Get up! Go on! I didn't say you could sit down.

John If you want me to stand you will have to help me.

Josh pauses, is not sure what to do.

Josh Bloody weirdo. Everyone thinks you're weird. You'll have to move. You'll have to get out of this street. Nobody wants you here.

John I think you are probably right.

Josh I'm going now. But this is not the end of it.

John No, I am sure you are right.

Josh goes to go.

Do you want a torch? A proper torch?

Josh What?

John The street lights are still off.

Josh I can see in the dark, me.

John Stop it.

Josh What?

John Stop this. I know who you are.

Josh What?

John I'm not stupid. You come in the video shop. You're the boy from next door. The boy who won't eat my mother's sweets. (*He laughs.*)

Josh You're scared of me.

John How can I be scared of you? You're just the little boy from next door. Used to ride your bike on the pavements.

Josh Watch me, did you?

John I saw you. I didn't watch you. Joshua, isn't it? How old are you? Twelve, thirteen?

Josh I'm fourteen.

John Come on. I'll take you home.

Josh Don't touch me, you perv.

John Don't do this, Joshua.

Josh I haven't done anything wrong.

John Take that thing off. There's no need to hide your face. I know exactly who you are.

John takes off the balaclava. Josh resists. John holds Josh to himself.

Josh (*a little boy suddenly*) I'm very tired.

John You don't know who to be, do you? Poor, poor boy. You don't know who to be.

Josh (*innocent*) I want to go to bed.

Louisa enters the house. She walks through the rooms, looking for Barnaby.

Louisa Barnaby?

Louisa enters BEDROOM ONE. *The baby is in a sling. Elsie gets her hammer out.*

Elsie Keep away from me! I'll beat you to a pulp! I'll knock your block off! I'll rip out your insides!

Louisa Ahh – stop! Please stop! I'm not trying to hurt you. Please – there's been some mistake.

Elsie looks at her in some confusion.

Elsie Mother?

Louisa I'm sorry – I thought –

Elsie Mother! You've come to me.

Elsie reaches out and takes hold of her. John lets go of Josh.

John Shsh. It's over now. Come on. I'll talk to your parents.

Josh I'm not going back there.

John Yes you are.

Josh You can say what you like. They don't care. They don't give a shit.

John Come on, I'm taking you home.
John and Josh exit.

SCENE FIFTEEN

In BEDROOM ONE *Louisa extricates herself from Elsie.*

Elsie Does this mean that I'm dying?

Louisa No.

Elsie I didn't want to die alone.

Louisa You're not dying.

Elsie I'm not? Oh.

Louisa No.

Elsie Oh.

Louisa I'm looking for my husband.

Elsie My son is downstairs. But you won't want him. He's not the marrying kind.

Louisa I didn't hear anybody downstairs.

Elsie Oh dear. I don't want to die without knowing he's all right. He's had a bit of trouble, you see. Through no fault of his own. He's a good boy. Never found his feet, that's all. He was a sensitive little boy, cried at the wind. My mother said, 'He's cowed, that child,' and I took it to heart, you see. I didn't know what I was doing. I pushed him too hard. Wanted him to stick up for himself.

Louisa I'm sure you did your best.

Elsie Did I?

The baby makes a little noise.

What's that?

Louisa The baby. She must be waking up. I'm in the wrong house. The door was open and I assumed – he must be on the other side.

Elsie Maybe my John's there too. I don't know what happened to him. He's not dead, is he?

Brian wakes up. He gets up and goes downstairs and gets the Calor gas heater from the KITCHEN. *Brian goes about setting up the Calor gas heater in the* LOUNGE. *He is fully absorbed and starts to whistle to himself as he sets it up. It cheers him up.*

Louisa Do you want to come with me? We'll find them together.

Elsie Yes, I'd like that.

Louisa I'm afraid I'm very slow.

Elsie It'll be a case of the blind and the blind then. (*Elsie places the hammer under the bed.*) Lead me through the forest, dear.

Louisa and Elsie start to walk through the house.

SCENE SIXTEEN

Everyone re-enters or walks around the house. Brian goes and gets the kettle from the KITCHEN. *He puts it on the Calor gas heater. There is music. They all wander lost around the house. They bump into things. They carry on. They all make their way to the* LOUNGE.

In the KITCHEN *Janet re-enters. She goes to the* STUDY, *a tiny knock.*

Janet Josh?

She takes a deep breath, enters, sees there is no one there. At the same time, Barnaby enters BEDROOM ONE.

Barnaby Louisa? (*He sees the bed and the Moses basket are empty.*)

Janet Josh! My little boy? Where's my little boy?

Barnaby Louisa! The baby? Where's the baby?

He starts to search for them – he goes to the BATHROOM *first.*

Janet Where's my little baby boy gone?

Janet goes into the LOUNGE, *passes Brian.*

Josh's gone –

Brian is warming his hands on the Calor gas heater.

Brian What?

Janet Where the fuck is he, you halfwit? Josh? Josh, Brian!

Janet runs back into the STUDY. *John enters the* LOUNGE *with Josh. From now on – all the dialogue starts to overlap.*

Brian Josh! He's here.

Janet Where have you been?

John He was wandering about outside. I've brought him home.

Janet Outside? You were outside? I didn't see you. Are you all right?

John He's fine.

Janet You're from next door, are you?

Brian Live with your mother?

Janet Josh, are you sure you're all right?

Josh I'm all right, all right!

Brian What happened to you?

John Tell them.

Janet (*urgent*) Josh?

Josh Nothing happened. Get off me. I'm going to bed.

Brian Yes, all right, son.

Josh exits. A pause. He goes to his STUDY. *First of all he stands before his computer, a little lost. Then, during the next, he takes his clothes off ready for bed, until he's down to his underpants. At the same time, Elsie and Louisa enter the* LOUNGE.

John I'm John Wrentmore.

Brian and Janet hang back from him slightly.

Elsie John! What happened to you, son? What did he do to you?

John (*evasive*) We'll talk about it later. This is my mother, Elsie Wrentmore.

Brian Mrs Wrentmore.

Elsie Don't look at him like that.

Janet I beg your pardon.

Elsie It may have come to your notice that my son has been wrongly accused of indecent acts with minors. But it wasn't him, you see. He happened to slightly resemble another man whose picture was printed in the paper. But as his mother I could have told them straight off that John doesn't have such a square jaw. He has always had what I call a weak jaw. He is prone to fat there. Besides, my John is a thoroughly decent man.

Pause.

It's better said, John. Get it out in the open. Stop folk whispering in corners. He has also admitted to me this evening that he is a homosexual.

John Yes, all right, Mother.

Elsie There's nothing wrong with it. It's perfectly normal. Sooner people acknowledge that the better, in my book.

Pause.

Louisa I'm Louisa, from next door, other side. I was looking for my husband.

Janet Yes. He was here. He was here all right.

Pause. Louisa and Janet look at each other. Barnaby enters, sees Louisa.

Barnaby Louisa. Are you all right? Is the baby –?

Louisa looks at him.

Louisa Your face has changed.

Barnaby What?

They look at each other strangely.

Louisa (*quiet, intense*) Where were you? We were on our own – what happened, Barnaby? What the fuck happened?

Barnaby (*evasive*) We'll talk about it later.

The baby gurgles.

Brian It's the little baby with no name!

Pause.

Janet Why don't you sit? All of you should sit. Please sit. Sit! There may be a power cut but that's no reason not to . . . It's not often we get to meet the neighbours!

They all sit. There are awkward, muttered mini-introductions.

Louisa Barnaby, this is Elsie and her son –

John John.

Brian I'm Brian.

Barnaby Brian and – (*He indicates Janet.*)

Janet Janet.

Louisa Yes, we've been –

The introductions peter out.

John Won't Joshua join us?

Brian Oh no, no.

Barnaby Has he slept through it all? Your boy?

Louisa You've got a little boy? How old is he?

Janet He's fourteen. He's very shy.

Brian He doesn't talk much – you know – that age.

Janet Although he said something just now, didn't he?

Brian Yes, first thing he's said in ages.

Janet Not that long, Brian.

Brian Six months.

Louisa Six months! He hasn't spoken in six months?

Brian Not to us.

Janet Oh, he talks on the phone and on the internet. Chats for hours. It's the age. It's a very difficult age.

They sit around the Calor gas heater.

Brian Well, this is civilised.

Pause.

We should go caravanning again.

Janet Hours putting up the awning in the mud and chemical toilets, no thank you very much.

Pause.

Barnaby I've got work tomorrow. First day back.

Pause.

Janet I should have gone back to work.

The dialogue begins to overlap. People talk in cross-currents – the whole room is talking. In the STUDY *we see Josh listening.*

John What did you do?

Janet I was only a secretary. But it got me out of the house.

At the same time:

Elsie What is it that you do?

Barnaby I'm an architect . . . I'm an architect.

Pause.

John I've been thinking we should convert the loft and get lodgers in. Language students.

Brian Language students?

John I just fancy a bit of life in the house, you know.

Louisa (*to Janet*) It's always a hard choice for women.

Elsie I loved my job.

Janet I've spent too much time in this house.

Brian You didn't want to go back. You told me you didn't want to go back.

Elsie I was a telephonist.

Janet But then I'm not what you call an alpha female.

John An architect, though! That must be a good job!

Janet No.

Louisa turns away from Janet, towards John.

John I don't think we could afford a loft conversion.

Elsie Fire, ambulance, police! The emergency services.

Louisa (*to John*) Barnaby could help you. You do loft conversions, don't you?

Brian We should do that. Convert the loft. For Josh.

Barnaby (*to Louisa*) Yes, although my speciality is glass domes.

Elsie Fire, ambulance, police! That was me!

John Glass domes?

Elsie Of course, it's all computerised these days. The emergency services.

Barnaby But nobody wants them. Being aspirational is – it's not helpful, I find.

Louisa That must have been an interesting job.

Elsie It's not the same. You need the comfort of a human voice.

Janet All day. Every day, just me and Josh. And Brian was away for long spells.

Brian No I can imagine there wouldn't be much call.

Elsie Glass domes? I wouldn't like that. People could just see in.

Brian We like our privacy.

Increasingly Janet talks to anyone and no one.

Janet I was starved of adult company. Nobody to talk to.

Barnaby I can do other stuff too.

Louisa (*to Janet*) I can feel like that. Trapped. It's the dependency.

Janet Brian wanted another one. But I had nothing left to give.

John (*to Barnaby*) Thank you. I might take you up on that.

Elsie (*to everyone and no one*) John runs the video store.

Janet I used to let him watch the TV. But just for a break.

Brian You've not long moved in, then?

Elsie John runs the video store.

Louisa Everyone deserves a little break.

Barnaby No. Louisa was seven months pregnant when we did.

Louisa Does he? We must join.

Janet I was sick every day of my pregnancy.

John Free joining. You just need proof of address – a utility bill, or driver's licence.

Brian It's a nice street, this.

Janet It was like my body was rejecting him.

John Mind you, I've met you now. I can wave that aside.

Elsie It's changed a lot, this street. Beyond all recognition.

Brian Do you like it?

Louisa So, John, you live with your mother?

Elsie It used to be different.

Barnaby Yes. I'm sure we'll settle. It's just been hard – with the baby. People seem very – friendly.

John After my dad died. She wasn't coping well.

Brian A woman was nice to me today. In the paper shop. Well, actually she trod on my foot, but then she was so mortified. She said, 'I'm so sorry, my love,' touched my arm, and I felt she really meant it.

Janet She didn't mean it. She doesn't know you. She wasn't nice to you. Why would she be nice to you if she didn't know you?

Brian Even if she didn't mean it, it made me feel better.

Silence.

Louisa When Jacob – our first child – died – when he died – a month after he died – I had this thing that I wanted to stop people – strangers and tell them – so I went into a shop – it was an office-stationery shop – you know – printing and stuff – and everyone was just going about their business and I said to the woman, 'I want to send a fax,' and she said, 'Okay,' and I said, 'I want it to read: "On the fourth of February my baby failed to wake up in his cot," and I want you to send it to every single number that you can think of.' And so she did. I was in the shop for two hours. She typed in the number and I pressed SEND until I had had enough. She did that for me.

Barnaby You've never told me that.

Louisa I'm sorry.

Barnaby There's no need to be sorry.

Janet Did she charge you?

Louisa What?

Janet For the faxes?

Louisa I paid her because even if she was humouring me I wanted to believe in it. I had to believe in it.

Pause.

SCENE SEVENTEEN

A lull in the conversation. The baby starts to grizzle. Louisa begins to sing. Her voice is pure and strong. Everyone is quiet. Janet in particular is moved by this. Josh gets up, walks to the LOUNGE *and listens. He does not enter.*

Louisa
Sleep, my child, and peace attend thee,
All through the night:
Guardian angels God will send thee,
All through the night;
Soft the drowsy hours are creeping,
Hill and vale in slumber sleeping,
I my loving vigil keeping,
All through the night.

Barnaby kisses Louisa on the lips. Janet watches. Josh goes back into the STUDY. *In Janet there is a growing sense of awfulness. She increases in voltage during the next. The kettle is also reaching boiling point.*

Elsie She's sleeping. Precious little dot!

Louisa That's nice.

Barnaby Yes.

Elsie They are precious little dots when they're like that.

Janet gets up.

Janet Will you excuse me?

Brian Janet?

Janet runs out, through the house. She finds the hammer under the bed in BEDROOM ONE. *She runs with the hammer, back through the* LOUNGE, *straight to the* STUDY. *Josh is sitting staring at a blank screen.*

Janet YOU LITTLE BASTARD! YOU LITTLE BASTARD! I'M TELLING YOU! GET OUT OF THE FUCKING WAY! I SAID GET THE FUCK OUT OF MY WAY.

She begins smashing up the computer. She is in a frenzy, screaming like a banshee. The others sit listening in the LOUNGE, *smiling weakly at each other.*

Josh No, Mum! Mum! Stop. What the fuck –?

Janet You can chat online to strangers in Kuala Lumpur but you don't have the grace to thank me for your dinner.

She continues smashing up the computer. Josh starts to cry. Brian enters.

Brian Janet! Stop it. Stop it. Give me back the hammer.

Janet GET OFF ME, YOU – LITTLE – FUCK –

Brian That's my hammer.

She is smashing the computer to bits.

Janet I KNOW WHAT YOU DO! I KNOW, JOSH! GOING OUT AT NIGHT. TERRORISING THE WORLD. YOU MONSTER! HOW COULD YOU! WHY ARE YOU LIKE THIS?! YOU LITTLE FUCK! YOU – EVIL – LITTLE – YOU – HOW COULD THIS HAPPEN?

She is screaming. Brian takes hold of her. Again the dialogue is a jumble.

Josh Mum – stop it – stop it – please –

Brian Janet! Not in front of everyone. Janet! Be quiet! SHUT UP, JANET.

Janet I can't do it! I can't live like this any more. I'm doing my best, but I can't do it any more.

Josh Thank you for my dinner, Mum! Thank you for my dinner!

Janet You've got to help me! Somebody's got to help me.

Brian I will. I will help you. Give me the hammer, there's a good girl.

Janet does so. She is shaking all over. Brian holds her a minute, then she shakes him off, pulls herself together. She walks back to the LOUNGE. *Brian stays with Josh in the study.*

Josh Dad! She broke my computer. She went ballistic. It's fucked. It's totally fucked.

Brian You shouldn't upset your mother.

Josh I didn't do anything – I didn't mean to – I'm sorry – I'm trying. Dad . . . Daddy. I'm trying.

Brian I know you are.

Josh hugs his dad. Brian is made supremely uncomfortable by the hug. Janet enters the lounge.

Janet Sorry about that.

John That's okay.

Janet I'd rather we carried on as if nothing had happened.

In the STUDY *Brian is awkward that his son has next to no clothes on. He hangs back from him. Brian pats Josh on the shoulders.*

Brian Never mind, son. Let's get some clothes on you, eh? Let's find your jim-jams. Clean your teeth and get to bed.

In the LOUNGE *Janet takes off the boiling kettle.*

Janet Cup of tea, anyone?

SCENE EIGHTEEN

Suddenly the lights come back on. The TV and music come back on everywhere. Chaos! A rush homewards. They speak all at once in a continuous stream.

John Oh!

Louisa The lights!

Brian The power's back on!

Elsie Thank God!

Barnaby There you go!

Janet Power's back on.

Brian starts to pick up the bits of computer.

John They must have fixed it.

Elsie Let's get home, John.

Josh sits down, a little lost in the light, dazed by it.

Brian I'd better just check on your mother.

Brian goes back into the LOUNGE. *During the next, Josh curls up in the* STUDY *to go to sleep.*

Louisa We ought to get home!

Barnaby I've got work tomorrow!

John What time is it?

Barnaby It's (*actual time*).

Elsie My programme won't have finished.

They all start to drift away to other rooms. To the light.

Barnaby We should get back.

Elsie They're putting the weather girl in solitary confinement tonight . . .

They have all gone . . .

Janet We must do this again. (*Janet turns off the Calor gas heater.*) Not wait for a power cut for the next time.

SCENE NINETEEN

Barnaby and Louisa to BEDROOM ONE, *where they lower the lights and get the baby ready for bed. John to* BEDROOM TWO – *on the way he picks up the sleeping tablets from* BEDROOM ONE, *goes to the second bedroom, where he switches off the TV and gets ready for bed. Elsie to the* BATHROOM, *where she washes her face, cleans her teeth, switches off the shower. Janet switches the TV off, sits. Brian leaves the* STUDY *and walks back into the* LOUNGE. *In* BEDROOM TWO, *John looks at the bottle of pills. Pours them out on the counterpane. Considers them. In the* LOUNGE *Janet sits in a daze. Brian enters.*

Janet We ought to ring the police.

Brian What for?

Janet Tonight. What happened tonight. Are you going to ring them, Brian? Please?

Pause. Brian picks the phone up. He does not dial. Janet watches him.

Brian Hello, officer, this is Brian Wheeler. Yes. I am ringing to tell you . . . I am ringing to tell you that I am under my wife's spell. My wife Janet and my son Joshua. Joshua – our little boy. Our son. And that anything else that happened tonight – we are going to black it out. I would rather black it out and act as if nothing happened. Okay?

Janet Yes.

Brian Thank you, officer. (*He puts the phone down. Pause.*)

Janet We won't need rewiring, then?

Brian No.

Janet It was the whole street after all.

Brian Yes . . . You've turned the tele off.

Janet It's only the news again.

Pause. Brian switches the TV back on. The news. He yawns.

Brian Feel like I could sleep a hundred years.

The headlines start. Janet mutes the sound but the images continue. She lays a hand on Brian – strokes his head. During this, John refills the pill bottle. He has decided not to take them tonight.

Janet Once upon a time, there was a man killed his whole family. He killed them while they were sleeping. And nobody could fathom out why. Only he knew why – he killed them because he loved them. He couldn't show it any other way, you see. He'd forgotten all the other ways. Things had got so bad he thought that it would be better to take them with him. It seemed the bravest thing to do . . . In his mind . . . he thought . . . they'd be happy ever after . . .

Brian Yes.

Janet You sleep, love . . . Think I'll have a bite to eat.

Brian smiles, closes his eyes. She leaves; as she does, she scratches her arm.

(*absently, to herself*) This mole's started to itch.

Brian does not hear her. She exits, goes to the kitchen.

At the same time Elsie exits from the BATHROOM *and goes to see John in* BEDROOM TWO.

In BEDROOM TWO *John is in bed. All the pills are back in the bottle. Elsie enters. She carries a fresh bandage with her.*

Elsie I've had my wash.

John Good.

Elsie Just checking on you.

John (*doing so*) I'm going straight to sleep. I'm taking a pill.

Elsie Are you going to tell me what happened tonight, son?

John There's nothing to tell. Really. I just need to sleep.

Pause.

Elsie Let me change that sling for you, before you go to sleep. Sit up.

John I'm all right.

She helps him out of his sling. Passively he lets her do it.

In BEDROOM ONE *Louisa places the baby in the cot.*

Barnaby What happened? What happened while I was away?

Pause.

Louisa Nothing happened.

Barnaby Nothing happened?

Louisa The lights came back on and you came back, that is what happened.

Barnaby Yes.

Louisa She's still asleep. Good girl.

Barnaby Dot. Little Dot.

Louisa You see, it came to us.

Barnaby I think she might live, Lou. We hadn't considered that. It might be the worst that happens to us. She might just live.

Pause. They look at her.

Louisa Go to sleep now. You've got work tomorrow. I'm going to have a shower first. Relax me. I'll turn the light off.

Barnaby No, leave it on. Leave it on, till you come to bed.

She kisses him, exits with her dressing gown. He checks on the baby one last time.

In the KITCHEN *Janet looks in the fridge absently, tries to find something to eat. Takes something out and pops it in the microwave. She scratches the mole on her arm. A thought and she walks to the* STUDY.

In the BATHROOM *Louisa goes to the shower. Switches it on. Waits for it to heat up. Stands cleaning her teeth.*

In the STUDY *Janet stands outside the door to Josh's room. Josh is nodding off to sleep.*

Janet Josh? I'll get you another one.

Josh rouses himself and smiles, gets up, switches his music on, quiet. Janet goes back into the kitchen. She gets the magnifying glass out of the drawer and starts inspecting her mole.

In BEDROOM TWO *Elsie changes John's sling.*

Elsie The darkest hour is just before dawn.

John Yes.

Elsie And tomorrow is another day.

In the LOUNGE *Brian clutches his heart. He appears to be in the throes of a heart attack.*

In BEDROOM ONE *Barnaby is falling asleep in bed – his vigil finally over.*

Barnaby Dot. Dot. Dot.

He starts to nod off. The music grows. He wakes himself up. The lights lower and raise three times as his head nods and then jolts up. The fourth time, he is asleep. The music reaches a crescendo, stops.

Blackout on all the rooms.